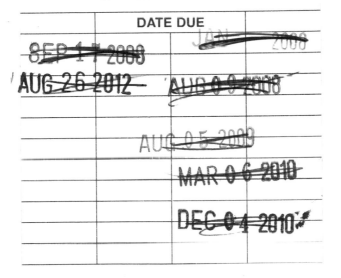

DATE DUE

SEP 17 2008	JAN 2008	
AUG 26 2012	AUG 09 2008	
	AUG 05 2009	
	MAR 06 2010	
	DEC 04 2010	

MONKEY
A Superhero Tale of China
— Aaron Shepard —

"Here I am, only four hundred years old," said the Monkey King, "and I've already reached the heights of greatness. What is left to hope and strive for? What can be higher than a king?"

"Your Majesty," said the gibbon carefully, "we have ever been grateful for that time four centuries ago when you hatched from the stone, wandered into our midst, and found for us this hidden cave behind the waterfall. We made you our king as the greatest honor we could bestow. Still, I must tell you that kings are not the highest of beings."

"They're not?" said the Monkey King.

"No, Your Majesty. Above them are gods, who dwell in Heaven and govern Earth. Then there are Immortals, who have gained great powers and live forever. And finally there are Buddhas and Bodhisattvas, who have conquered illusion and escaped rebirth."

"Wonderful!" cried the Monkey King. "Maybe I can become all three!" He considered a moment, then said, "I think I'll start with the Immortals. I'll search the earth till I've found one, then learn to become one myself!"

Also by Aaron Shepard

Chapter Books, Novels, and Collections

Timothy Tolliver and the Bully Basher
Mad, Magic, and Marvelous (forthcoming)

Picture Books

King o' the Cats
The Princess Mouse: A Tale of Finland
Master Man: A Tall Tale of Nigeria
Lady White Snake: A Tale From Chinese Opera
The Sea King's Daughter: A Russian Legend
The Baker's Dozen: A Saint Nicholas Tale
The Magic Brocade: A Tale of China
Forty Fortunes: A Tale of Iran
The Crystal Heart: A Vietnamese Legend
Master Maid: A Tale of Norway
The Maiden of Northland: A Hero Tale of Finland
The Gifts of Wali Dad: A Tale of India and Pakistan
The Enchanted Storks: A Tale of Bagdad
The Legend of Slappy Hooper: An American Tall Tale
The Legend of Lightning Larry
Savitri: A Tale of Ancient India
Two-Eyes (forthcoming)

MONKEY

A Superhero Tale of China

Aaron Shepard

Skyhook Press

Published from Los Angeles and Olympia, Washington

Hardcover
ISBN-13:   978-0-938497-25-7
ISBN-10:   0-938497-25-1
Paperback
ISBN-13:   978-0-938497-26-4
ISBN-10:   0-938497-26-X

Library of Congress Control Number: 2004093990

Ages 10 and up

1.0

For Kwan Yin

Contents

How to Say the Names

Bodhisattva	BO-dee-SOT-va
Buddha	BOO-da
Kwan Yin	KWON YIN
Lao Tzu	LOW (rhymes with "cow") TZOO
Siddhartha	sid-AR-ta
Subodhi	soo-BO-dee
Yama	YOM-a

Prologue:
From Out of Stone

Far across the Eastern Sea, on the island called the Mountain of Flowers and Fruit, a magic boulder had sat on the mountain's peak since the creation of the world. Bathed in the energies of Earth and Heaven, quickened by the light of Sun and Moon, the stone became fertile, and at last cracked open to release its young.

From this stone egg emerged a full-grown monkey. As it gazed about and above, golden light shot from its eyes to the farthest reaches of Heaven and Earth.

* * *

High above in Heaven, the Jade Emperor, Ruler of Heaven and Earth, was startled by the rays of light reaching his Celestial Throne.

"See what's causing that," he ordered his chief minister, the Spirit of the Great White Planet Venus.

The Great White Planet went to look out the East Gate of Heaven and soon returned with his report. "Your Majesty, a stone has given birth to a monkey. The rays of light came from its eyes. But now that the monkey has taken food, the light is fading."

The Jade Emperor sighed. "Only a monkey, is it? Well, we have important business here. A monkey is no concern of ours."

* * *

Elsewhere in Heaven, Lord Lao Tzu, Supreme Patriarch of the Way, was refining Elixir of Life, when just for a moment the golden rays penetrated his alchemy laboratory.

"Such a powerful beam!" murmured Lao Tzu in wonder. "The one who produced it will surely become an Immortal!"

* * *

Far off in the Western Paradise, the Buddha paused in his blessed discourse to his disciples as the rays of light shone into the temple hall. He closed his eyes a moment in silent meditation, then turned to Kwan Yin, Most Compassionate Bodhisattva and Goddess of Mercy.

"A remarkable creature has been born: a monkey, yet not an ordinary one. I see he is destined to become an enlightened being, a true Buddha. Yet before he does, he will offer us no end of mischief."

And so saying, he resumed his blessed discourse.

1

The Birthday Quest

On the Mountain of Flowers and Fruit, in the Heavenly Cave of the Water Curtain, the island monkeys were feasting to celebrate the birthday of their king. But the Monkey King himself sat there gloomily.

"What's wrong, Your Majesty?" asked an old gibbon.

"Here I am, only four hundred years old," said the Monkey King, "and I've already reached the heights of greatness. What is left to hope and strive for? What can be higher than a king?"

"Your Majesty," said the gibbon carefully, "we have ever been grateful for that time four centuries ago when you hatched from the stone, wandered into our midst, and found for us this hidden cave behind the waterfall. We made you our king as the greatest honor we could bestow. Still, I must tell you that kings are not the highest of beings."

"They're not?" said the Monkey King.

"No, Your Majesty. Above them are gods, who dwell in Heaven and govern Earth. Then there are Immortals, who have gained great powers and live forever. And finally there are Buddhas and Bodhisattvas, who have conquered illusion and escaped rebirth."

"Wonderful!" cried the Monkey King. "Maybe I can become all three!" He considered a moment, then said, "I think I'll start with the Immortals. I'll search the earth till I've found one, then learn to become one myself!"

The very next morning, the Monkey King ordered a pine raft to be built and loaded with fruit for the journey. Then he took leave of his cheering subjects, floated downstream to the island's edge, and started across the great sea.

2
Meeting the Master

On the Mountain of Heart and Mind, the Monkey King stood before a double door in the mountainside. Beside it was a huge stone tablet carved in ancient characters.

DIVINE CAVE OF THE THREE STARS

"This is the place!" said the Monkey King. "Right where the woodcutter told me. I just hope I look all right in these human clothes." He glanced down at what he'd gathered on his journey—black boots, red robe, and yellow sash.

Just then, one of the doors opened and a young man peered out at him. "You can't be the one!" he exclaimed in horror.

"What one?" asked the Monkey King.

"My master, the Patriarch Subodhi, just mounted the dais to deliver the day's discourse. But instead of starting, he told me to open the door, because someone had come who wished to study the Way."

"That's me!" said the Monkey King.

"You don't say!" said the young man, laughing. "Then come along."

They walked down a stone corridor and into a large chamber, where thirty or forty disciples faced a dais made of jade. Sitting cross-legged on the platform was a man who looked as old as Heaven, yet strong and healthy. His flowing beard trailed away behind him.

"Master!" cried the Monkey King, dropping to his knees and knocking his head on the floor. "Please accept this humble seeker as your disciple!"

"Humble, is it?" said the Patriarch. "We'll see about that! But tell me, what is your name?"

"I have no name, Master, for I had no parents to give me one. I was born from a magic stone."

"Most unusual," said the Patriarch thoughtfully. "Well, what if I name you 'Monkey'?"

"Master, what an ingenious idea! It fits me perfectly!"

"Then 'Monkey' it is," said the Patriarch. "And for now, you may stay and learn with the others—just as long as you keep out of trouble!"

* * *

So Monkey became a student of the Way. Each day, he studied scriptures, discussed doctrine, and listened to the discourse of the Patriarch. The rest of the time, he swept the cave, helped in the vegetable garden and orchard, gathered firewood, and carried water from the stream. Days went by, then weeks, then months, then years.

One day during the Patriarch's discourse, Monkey grew so excited that he could not contain himself. With his eyes closed, he got up on all fours and began leaping and turning.

"Stop that!" roared the Patriarch. "Monkey, why are you prancing about?"

"Forgive me, Master!" said Monkey. "I was so happy to hear your words, I danced without knowing it!"

"Is that so!" said the Patriarch, looking at Monkey thoughtfully. "You've been here seven years now, I believe. Tell me, what branch of the Way do you wish to learn from me?"

"Master," said Monkey, "you know how ignorant I am. Anything you want to teach me is fine."

"What if I teach you the Way of the Seventy-Two Changes? You'll then be able to turn yourself into anything you want."

"Wonderful!" said Monkey.

So the Patriarch whispered into Monkey's ear.

For three months, Monkey practiced the techniques in private. Then one day, as he walked back from his chores in the orchard, the Patriarch came up to him.

"Monkey, how are you doing with those tidbits I taught you?"

"Just fine, Master," said Monkey. "I can now accomplish all of the Seventy-Two Changes. But tell me, Master, will this make me immortal?"

"Not likely!" said the Patriarch.

"Then I beg you to teach me more."

"All right," said the Patriarch. "What about Cloud Soaring? You'll then be able to travel quickly wherever you want."

"Marvelous!" said Monkey.

The Patriarch explained, "When Immortals or Buddhas or gods want to travel great distances, they ride on magic clouds. They rise to the cloud by stamping one foot, and stamp it again to move the cloud forward. But you're built differently. So instead, let's try the Cloud Somersault."

Then the Patriarch taught Monkey how to somersault high into the air, land on a magic cloud, and propel it across the sky with more somersaults.

Another three months passed while Monkey practiced. Soon he could travel for hundreds of miles with each somersault. Then one day the Patriarch paused in his discourse and addressed Monkey again from the dais.

"Monkey, how are you doing with that little trick I taught you?"

"Very well, Master. But tell me, will this make me immortal?"

"I should say not!"

"Then please, Master, teach me more!"

The Patriarch jumped from the dais and stalked angrily up to Monkey. "You greedy creature! Will you never be satisfied? Will you never stop demanding?"

He thumped Monkey on the head three times. Then, with his hands held behind his back, he stomped into his private chamber and slammed the door.

"Stupid ape!" yelled one of the disciples. "You've upset the Master!"

"Yes," said another, "and who knows when he'll come out again!"

But Monkey just sat there grinning.

Late that night, Monkey crept from the disciples' sleeping place, out the front door of the cave, and around to the back. There he found the Patriarch's door left open a crack.

"Come in, Monkey," came the Patriarch's voice.

Monkey slipped inside. In the candlelight, he saw the Patriarch sitting cross-legged on his cot.

The Patriarch smiled. "I see you understood my secret signs."

"Yes, Master. I knew that hitting me three times meant to come here in the third watch of the night. And holding your hands behind you meant to use the back door. I came just as you instructed."

"In that case," said the Patriarch, "it's your destiny to learn the Way of Immortality. Come close, my disciple, and hear the secrets of Eternal Life."

And so the Patriarch revealed his precious wisdom. But what he said must not be written here.

* * *

For three years Monkey practiced the secret techniques. His body grew hard and enduring and full of powerful energies. Then one day, he was sitting with the other disciples outside the cave.

"Monkey," said one of them, "what is that nonsense about the 'Seventy-Two Changes'? Can you really turn yourself into something else?"

"I certainly can," said Monkey proudly.

"We won't believe it till we see it," said another.

"Then just watch this," said Monkey. He called out, "Change!" And there in place of Monkey stood a unicorn!

"Bravo! Bravo!" yelled the students. They cheered and applauded as Monkey changed back and took a bow.

Just then, the Patriarch Subodhi burst from the cave. "What's all this noise?" he shouted. "Don't you know that followers of the Way never shout?"

"We're sorry, Master," said Monkey. "I was just showing them one of my changes."

The Patriarch turned white. "Away, all of you—except Monkey!"

When they were alone, the Patriarch turned on his disciple. "Is that how you use your powers—to show off? Don't you realize the others will be jealous? They're sure to come and demand your secrets. And if you refuse, they may seek revenge!"

"Master, I'm sorry!" said Monkey. "I didn't think!"

"Well, I won't punish you," said the Patriarch. "But you're not safe here any longer, so you'll have to leave."

"Master, where would I go?" said Monkey in alarm.

"That's your business," said the Patriarch. "But on your way, you'd better pick up a magic weapon for protection. The Dragon King of the Eastern Sea might have something useful."

"But, Master," said Monkey with tears in his eyes, "how can I leave without repaying all your kindness?"

"Don't do me any favors," said the Patriarch. "Once you're gone, you're bound to land in serious trouble. Just keep my name out of it, and don't you dare tell anyone you're my disciple!"

"Master, I promise," said Monkey. "Good-bye, Master." Then he somersaulted into the air, landed on a magic cloud, and flew off, head over heels.

3
The Dragon King's Gift

At the bottom of the Eastern Sea, before the green jade palace of the Dragon King, Monkey marched up to a cowrie shell gate where a Dragon Captain stood guard. The captain stared in amazement.

"I'm here to see the Dragon King," declared Monkey. "Tell him it's the Monkey King from the Mountain of Flowers and Fruit. And be quick about it!"

"Yes, sir!" said the captain, saluting smartly.

In a few minutes, the captain was ushering Monkey into the throne room.

"Welcome, brother," said the Dragon King stiffly. "How kind of you to pay this most unexpected visit."

"Don't mention it," said Monkey.

"Tell me, brother," said the Dragon King, "how did you gain the art of living under water?"

"I've studied the magic arts of the Way for many years," said Monkey. "In fact, that's why I'm here! Now that I'm an Immortal, I need a magic weapon to match my abilities. Can you spare one?"

"An Immortal!" remarked the Dragon King. "Well now, perhaps I can find one for you. Captain, bring out the Scimitar of the Waning Moon."

The captain fetched a large scimitar. Monkey took it and made a few passes at the air. "Too light! Too light!"

The Dragon King laughed. "Brother, you must be joking. That scimitar weighs nearly a hundred pounds!"

"It just doesn't feel right," said Monkey.

The Dragon King looked somewhat alarmed. "Captain, bring out the Battle-Ax of the Noonday Sun."

The captain brought it out, and Monkey swung it a few times. "Still too light. Way too light!"

Now the Dragon King looked really frightened. "Brother, that weapon is over a thousand pounds!"

"I need more weight!" declared Monkey. "Don't you have anything heavier?"

"I assure you," said the Dragon King, "that's the heaviest weapon in the palace!"

Just then, the Dragon Queen entered from a door behind the throne, bowed graciously to Monkey, then spoke low to the king. "This monkey is no ordinary fellow. Perhaps you should give him the giant stamping rod in your treasury."

"That old piece of scrap?" whispered the Dragon King. "What could he do with it?"

"That's his concern, not ours," hissed the queen. "Just give it to him and get him out of the palace!"

The queen bowed graciously to Monkey and took her leave.

The Dragon King cleared his throat nervously. "I remember now that in my treasury is an iron rod once belonging to Yu the Great. He used it to pound down the beds of the rivers and seas in the time of the Great Flood. Perhaps it will meet your needs."

"Bring it out and we'll have a look," said Monkey.

"I'm afraid that's impossible," said the Dragon King. "It weighs ten tons, and not one of us can lift it! We'll have to go ourselves to see it."

The Dragon King led Monkey across a courtyard and into the treasury, then pointed out a pillar of black iron. It was twenty feet high and as thick as a barrel, and both ends were tipped with gold. As Monkey approached, the pillar began to glow.

"It likes me!" said Monkey.

He examined the pillar closely and found characters inscribed near the bottom band.

CELESTIAL STAFF OF THE OBEDIENT IRON

Monkey put both hands on the pillar and lifted it. The Dragon King gasped.

"The weight seems right," said Monkey. "If only it were smaller."

At once, the staff shrank to 15 feet and became thinner too.

"Wonderful!" said Monkey. "It really is obedient! But even smaller would be nice."

It shrank to 10 feet.

"Almost there," said Monkey.

Five feet.

"Perfect!" said Monkey. He hefted the staff and declared, "It weighs the same as before!"

As they returned through the courtyard, Monkey tried some practice thrusts and parries. The Dragon King turned pale and jumped out of range. "Brother, please be careful!"

Monkey said, "I believe this little beauty will do anything I want." He called out, "Grow!" Both Monkey and the staff shot up to over two hundred feet tall.

"Take this! And that!" he shouted, swinging at an imaginary foe. The water swirled so furiously, it nearly swept away the Dragon King.

Then Monkey called "Shrink!" Monkey and staff returned swiftly to normal height. "Smaller!"—and the staff alone became the size of a needle. Monkey lodged it safely in his ear.

He turned to the Dragon King, who was now trembling violently. "Thank you, brother! You've been a most gracious host!"

"Don't mention it," said the Dragon King.

And with a leap and a somersault, Monkey was gone.

4
Death's Domain

On the surface of the Eastern Sea, not far from the Dragon King's palace, Monkey landed lightly on a barren rock that jutted above the waves. Stretching himself out on it, he yawned and then studied the sky.

"Now that I'm an Immortal, I think I'll fly up to Heaven and become a god as well. But that's all after a good nap."

He closed his eyes and quickly drifted into sleep.

All at once Monkey felt himself jerked to his feet. Two men were clutching his elbows. One man had the face of a horse, the other had the head of an ox.

Horse Face held an official document, which he studied closely. "Is your name Monkey?"

"That's right," said Monkey, in a daze.

"All right," said Ox Head, "get moving!"

They started to drag him off. Stumbling once, Monkey happened to glance back. There he saw himself, still lying on the ground!

They rounded the rock and started across a desolate plain. The sea was nowhere in sight. "Where is this?" he asked. "And how did I get here?"

"He wants to know how he got here!" snorted Horse Face.

"You got here the same way as everyone!" said Ox Head.

After a while they came to the wall of a city. Above the gate was an iron placard with characters inlaid in gold.

DEMON GATE OF THE LAND OF DARKNESS

"Land of Darkness?" exclaimed Monkey, at last coming fully awake. "But that's the realm of Yama, Lord of the Dead! I don't belong here!"

"That's what they all say!" said Horse Face.

"But I'm an Immortal!" protested Monkey. "I've gone beyond death!"

"Tell it to the judge!" said Ox Head.

"All right, I will!" said Monkey, snatching his staff from its hiding place in his ear. "Grow!" he cried, and in half a moment he was swinging five feet of it.

"We didn't mean it!" cried Horse Face, fleeing through the gate.

"Can't you take a joke?" said Ox Head, racing after.

Monkey followed them in, still swinging his staff. The demons of the city were terrified, and not one of them dared get in his way. By the time Monkey reached the Palace of Darkness, Lord Yama and the other nine Judges of the Dead were waiting on the steps.

"Sir, what seems to be the trouble?" asked Yama nervously.

"The trouble?" said Monkey. "The trouble is you've brought me here!"

"But sir, I assure you," said Yama, "you will be judged fairly and punished—I mean, re-educated—strictly according to your past deeds. Then when the evil you've done has been avenged—I mean, corrected—you'll be returned to the Land of Light for a brand new life."

"I don't want to be reborn!" said Monkey. "I don't want to die in the first place! Don't you realize I'm an Immortal?"

"An Immortal!" said Yama in consternation. "There must be some mistake!"

"Exactly!" said Monkey. "I demand to see the Register of Life and Death."

Yama led him into the Hall of Darkness, where a clerk dragged out several musty volumes. Monkey searched till he found his name.

"Writing brush!" commanded Monkey, and the clerk gave him one dipped in ink. Monkey blotted his name from the register. "That should do it," he said.

"This is most irregular!" protested Yama.

"Tell it to the judge!" said Monkey. He slammed the book shut and rushed out. Then he made his way back to the city wall, swinging his staff as he went.

Just outside the gate, Monkey tripped and fell rolling. When he opened his eyes, he was back on the rock in the Eastern Sea.

"Wonderful!" cried Monkey as he jumped to his feet. "Next stop: Heaven."

5
The Emperor of All

High above in Heaven, at the Cloud Palace of the Golden Doors, in the Hall of Divine Mist, the Jade Emperor, Ruler of Heaven and Earth, was having a bad day.

He had spent his whole morning stamping his official seal on documents promoting or demoting heavenly officials. In the afternoon his wife, the Lady Queen Mother, had demanded his help with the invitation list for the Grand Banquet of Immortal Peaches. And now both the Dragon King of the Eastern Sea and Yama, Lord of the Dead, stood before him complaining of some kind of monkey who had become immortal, with power enough to threaten them both.

"I'll see to it at once," said the Jade Emperor. "Now, both of you, please return to your kingdoms."

No sooner had the Dragon King and Yama left the hall than a lieutenant rushed in and bowed to the ground.

"Your Majesty, there's trouble at the East Gate. A talking monkey arrived there an hour ago and demanded entrance. Four of our guards engaged him in combat, but he is holding them all off with a simple staff."

"Indeed," said the Jade Emperor, raising an imperial eyebrow. "This must be the monkey Immortal that was reported to us." He turned to his commander-in-chief, the Heavenly General of Mighty Miracle. "Round up the twelve Thunder Generals and arrest the fiend."

But the Spirit of the Great White Planet Venus stepped forward and said, "Your Majesty, as your chief minister, I must point out that this monkey's deeds may not yet merit such a response. Would it not be better simply to invite him into Heaven and offer him a position? Then we could keep an eye on him and avoid further trouble."

"An excellent idea," said the Jade Emperor. "You may go at once to extend the invitation."

The Great White Planet soon returned with Monkey and bowed low before the Celestial Throne. "Your Majesty, I have brought the Immortal."

"Remarkable," said the Jade Emperor, looking Monkey up and down.

"Glad to meet you too!" said Monkey. "So, what's it like, running the universe?"

A gasp went up from the Great White Planet and from the other court officials. The Jade Emperor stared icily at Monkey. "In light of your primitive background and the recentness of your arrival, I will overlook your ignorance of court etiquette."

"Thank you, Your Majesty!" said Monkey. "I knew we'd get along."

"Now, in regard to a post," said the Jade Emperor, "my officials tell me the only current vacancy is as a supervisor in the Imperial Stables."

"Sounds important!" said Monkey. "I'll take it!"

"Very good," said the Jade Emperor. "Henceforth, your title shall be 'Protector of Horses.'"

"'Protector of Horses,'" said Monkey dreamily. "Thank you, Your Majesty!" And as the Great White Planet pulled him quickly from the hall, he called back, "You won't be sorry!"

"I'm not so sure about that," muttered the Jade Emperor.

6
Havoc in Heaven

At the Imperial Stables of the Jade Emperor, a banquet of welcome and congratulation was being held for the new Protector of Horses. In just a few weeks of Monkey's care, the thousand heavenly coursers and chargers had begun to grow sleek and muscular. The officials under him liked him as well, and so had gathered in his honor.

"What a wonderful feast!" said Monkey as he sampled all the dishes. "I certainly like the food here in Heaven!"

"This isn't bad," said his chief assistant wistfully. "Still, it's nothing compared to the food at the Grand Banquet of Immortal Peaches."

"What's that?" asked Monkey.

"Each year the Lady Queen Mother holds a banquet at the Pavilion of the Jade Pool. Her guests all dine on Immortal Peaches grown in her orchard. Each peach has ripened for nine thousand years and adds that many years to the life of the one who eats it. And for dessert, they have Pills of Immortality, made from Elixir of Life refined by Lord Lao Tzu in the Crucible of the Eight Trigrams. A single pill will guarantee eternal life."

"I can hardly wait!" said Monkey. "When is the banquet?"

"Today," said the assistant.

"But I haven't had an invitation," said Monkey.

"Of course not," said the assistant. "Your post is too low."

"What do you mean?" said Monkey in alarm. "I thought Protector of Horses was a high-ranking position."

"On the contrary," said the assistant. "It's so low, it has no rank at all!"

Monkey was stunned. "So that's what they think of me, is it? Me! The Monkey King! Well, I won't stand for it! I'll go to the banquet whether they want me or not!"

He rushed outside, somersaulted onto a cloud, and sped off.

* * *

At the Pavilion of the Jade Pool, servants ran about, busily setting the tables. From where he had landed nearby, Monkey could see trays loaded with Immortal Peaches, and bowls brimming with Pills of Immortality. There were also large pitchers filled with juice of jade, and heaping plates of delicacies like unicorn liver and phoenix marrow.

Monkey's mouth watered. "I won't bother waiting for the other guests," he said. "Change!"—and he became an exact image of the Spirit of the Great White Planet Venus.

Monkey stepped into the pavilion and announced in the chief minister's voice, "A command from the Jade Emperor! You are all to go to the Cloud Palace of the Golden Doors for further instructions."

"What in Heaven could that be about?" said the head steward. "All right, we'd better not dally." And all the servants rushed off.

As soon as Monkey was alone, he changed back to himself and started grabbing peaches right and left. They tasted so heavenly, he wanted to eat them all—but since there were so many, he took just a bite or two from each one. He guzzled the jade juice and bolted down whole plates of delicacies.

And he popped Pills of Immortality into his mouth like peanuts.

"At last!" he said. "A feast fit for a Monkey King!"

* * *

At the Cloud Palace of the Golden Doors, in the Hall of Divine Mist, the guests of the Lady Queen Mother had gathered to await the Grand Banquet of Immortal Peaches. Nearly all of the most important divinities were there, including ministers from all departments of the heavenly administration, heavenly generals, many star and constellation spirits, and a number of Bodhisattvas and Immortals. Seated beside the Jade Emperor and the Lady Queen Mother were Lord Lao Tzu, Supreme Patriarch of the Way, and Kwan Yin, Most Compassionate Bodhisattva and Goddess of Mercy.

As the Jade Emperor conversed with the guests, the head steward entered and bowed low before the Celestial Throne. "Your Majesty, your servants are assembled outside the hall, awaiting your instructions for the banquet."

"Instructions?" said the Jade Emperor. "I have none to give!"

"But, Your Majesty," said the steward, "the venerable Spirit of the Great White Planet Venus commanded us in your name to come and receive them!"

"The Great White Planet has been here the whole time, and I gave no such order!" The Jade Emperor turned to his commander-in-chief, the Heavenly General of Mighty Miracle. "Go at once to the Pavilion of the Jade Pool and find out what's behind this. And take along the twelve Thunder Generals, in case there's trouble."

* * *

At the Pavilion of the Jade Pool, Monkey had eaten as much as he possibly could and was patting his stomach in satisfaction. But a moment later he looked nervously at the scene around him.

"I don't think I'll win any friends this way!" he said. "I'd better clear out before I'm spotted."

But just then the Heavenly General of Mighty Miracle ran up with the twelve Thunder Generals. "Monstrous monkey!" he bellowed. "You've ruined the Grand Banquet of Immortal Peaches!"

"There's not much doubt about that!" said Monkey, with a sheepish grin. "But what are you going to do about it?"

"You sickening simian!" roared Mighty Miracle. "Have a taste of my battle-ax!"

Mighty Miracle rushed at Monkey, who grabbed his staff from his ear and called, "Grow!" Just in time, he blocked the swing of Mighty Miracle's ax.

"You'll have to do better than that!" said Monkey.

Mighty Miracle swung again and again, but Monkey parried every blow. Soon they were moving so fast, their arms were just a blur.

Mighty Miracle bellowed, "Let's see if you can face my magic powers! Grow!"—and he shot up to over a hundred feet tall.

"I know that trick too!" called Monkey. "Grow!"—and he was once more face to face with his opponent.

The noise of their battle was deafening, and their movements raised a wind that nearly blew away the twelve Thunder Generals. But neither could gain an advantage.

All at once Monkey cried, "Shrink!" and somersaulted into the air. At normal size, he sailed right by Mighty Miracle's battle-ax. He brought his staff down squarely on the Heavenly General's shoulder as he passed over it.

Mighty Miracle roared with pain, then quickly shrank to normal size and retreated.

Now the twelve Thunder Generals surrounded Monkey and attacked him with their battle-axes, swords, lances, halberds, maces, and scimitars. Monkey whirled like a top, countering every blow. But after a while he grew tired.

"This is hardly a fair fight!" he said. "But here's a trick you haven't seen yet!"

He yanked a dozen hairs from his tail, threw them in the air, and cried, "Change!" Each hair became a monkey that swung an iron staff against one of the Thunder Generals.

"Now I can take a break!" said Monkey. He put his staff away in his ear and stood grinning in the midst of the battle.

At that moment, the Imperial Chariot arrived at the pavilion with the Jade Emperor, the Lady Queen Mother, Lord Lao Tzu, and Kwan Yin.

The Jade Emperor was aghast. "What did I tell you! It's that fiendish monkey again!"

"Just look at my banquet!" cried the Lady Queen Mother. "It's a complete disaster!"

"Your Majesty," said Kwan Yin to the Jade Emperor, "it appears that your generals could use a bit of help in dealing with the Immortal. Will you permit me?"

"Most Compassionate Bodhisattva," said the Jade Emperor, "I am grateful for your offer. But I must point out that you have no weapon."

"I have this porcelain vase of willow twigs, which I always carry with me," replied Kwan Yin. "Allow me to show you how useful it can be."

Kwan Yin stamped her foot, rose a hundred feet in the air, and landed on a magic cloud. Then taking careful aim, she dropped her vase right onto Monkey's head.

Monkey dropped unconscious to the ground. The fighting monkeys at once changed back to hairs, returning to his tail.

Kwan Yin retrieved her vase and landed back in the chariot.

"Well done!" declared the Jade Emperor.

"It is not worth mentioning," replied the Bodhisattva.

The Heavenly General of Mighty Miracle came up. "Your Majesty, what are your wishes regarding the Protector of Horses?"

"Take him at once to the execution block," said the Jade Emperor. "Cut him into a thousand pieces!"

"Your Majesty," said Lord Lao Tzu, "I'm afraid such a punishment is no longer possible. After eating so many of my Pills of Immortality, his body must be as hard as a diamond. No weapon could pierce or even scratch it."

"Then what are we to do with him?" asked the Jade Emperor in dismay.

"Perhaps I can be of service," said Lao Tzu. "Hand him over to me, and I'll heat him in my Crucible of the Eight Trigrams. In just an hour his body will be consumed to ash— and at the same time, I can recover my elixir."

"I accept your kind and considerate offer," said the Jade Emperor. "We will return to the palace to await word of your success."

7
The Buddha's Bet

In the alchemy laboratory of the Cinnabar Palace, Lord Lao Tzu, Supreme Patriarch of the Way, dumped Monkey into the Crucible of the Eight Trigrams, clamped down the lid, and lifted the crucible onto the hearth.

"Stoke up the fire as high as you can," he told his assistant. "We'll need the greatest heat possible to refine this villain."

Meanwhile, Monkey was starting to come to. "What hit me?" he wondered, rubbing his sore head. "And where in Heaven have they taken me?"

He groped around in the dark. "It's some kind of porcelain pot, and it's getting warm! Are they trying to bake me? Or burn me to ashes? Well, I won't let them do it!"

Monkey pushed and kicked at the lid, but it wouldn't give. Then he took the miniature staff from his ear, held it pointing up, and said, "Grow!"

In a flash the staff enlarged to five feet, pushing against the bottom of the crucible and shattering the top. As Monkey jumped out, he knocked over the astonished Supreme Patriarch, sending him head over heels.

Monkey ran in a blind rage all the way from the Cinnabar Palace to the Cloud Palace of the Golden Doors, brandishing his staff at every heavenly official along the way. At the palace steps he found the Heavenly General of Mighty Miracle and the twelve Thunder Generals, who all grew pale at the sight of him.

"So you thought you could do away with the Monkey King!" shouted Monkey. "Well, here's a message for the Jade Emperor: I'm no longer the Protector of Horses. I'm now the Great Sage Equal to Heaven. And he's no longer the Jade Emperor, because I'm taking over! If he doesn't step down from the Celestial Throne, I'll come and pull him off it!"

* * *

In the Hall of Divine Mist, the Jade Emperor could hardly believe the message he had heard from the Heavenly General.

"The audacity of this wretched monkey knows no bounds!" he declared. "Gather as many soldiers as you need and wipe him out!"

"Your Majesty," said the Heavenly General uneasily, "I fear we are unable to do so. The creature is too powerful a fighter for any single warrior to defeat. And if we send great numbers against him, he can easily outdo us with an army made from the hairs of his body. Even if we capture him again, we have no way to destroy or imprison him."

"Just what are you telling me?" asked the Jade Emperor in amazement. "That I must give up my throne to this stinking monkey?"

"Your Majesty," said Kwan Yin, "I don't think it need come to that. There is still one who could defeat the rebellious Immortal and preserve your rule. Why not send to the Western Paradise and ask the assistance of the Buddha?"

The Jade Emperor said, "If the resources of Heaven are not enough to defeat this monster, I suppose I have no choice!"

Moments later, the Spirit of the Great White Planet Venus was speeding on a magic cloud out the West Gate of Heaven. It was not long before he reached the Western

Paradise, where he landed on the Mountain of Miracles and entered the Temple of the Thunderclap.

The Buddha listened closely to the message of the Great White Planet. Then he turned to his disciples. "Remain steadfast in your practice of meditation until my return."

* * *

Outside the Cloud Palace of the Golden Doors, Monkey marched up and down, swinging his staff, till his patience ran out.

"Time's up!" he yelled at the quaking Thunder Generals. "I'm coming in!"

But just as he stepped forward, a magic cloud landed in front of him. Off it stepped a huge man in the robe of a monk.

"What's this?" said Monkey. "Who are you, old monk, and why are you standing in my way?"

The man laughed. "I am Siddhartha, often called the Buddha. I am told you call yourself the Great Sage Equal to Heaven and even demand the Jade Emperor's place on the Celestial Throne."

"That's right," said Monkey. "He's been there long enough. Someone else should get a turn."

"The Jade Emperor," said the Buddha, "has been perfecting himself through four million lifetimes, for over two hundred million years. And you're not yet even fully human! What makes you think you're suited to rule Heaven and Earth?"

"I have great powers," said Monkey. "I've mastered the Seventy-Two Changes. And I can travel for hundreds of miles with a single somersault!"

"Indeed!" said the Buddha. "Then could you stand on the palm of my hand and somersault clear out of it?"

Monkey stared at the Buddha. "Enlightenment must have addled your brain! I just said I can somersault hundreds of miles. How could I not jump out of your palm?"

"Then wager with me," said the Buddha. "If you get off my palm with a single somersault, the Celestial Throne will be yours. I'll just tell the Jade Emperor to come live with me in the Western Paradise. But if you don't make it off my palm, you'll return to Earth and leave Heaven alone."

"You can make good on your promise?" asked Monkey.

"Certainly," said the Buddha.

"Then you're on!"

Monkey put away his staff and jumped onto the Buddha's palm, which was the size of a lotus leaf. Then he gave the mightiest leap of his life.

Head over heels Monkey tumbled through the air, spinning like a windmill for hundreds, thousands of miles. At last he came to five olive colored pillars reaching high into the sky.

"This must be the end of Heaven," he told himself, and he landed at the base of the middle pillar. "That bet wasn't hard to win. But I'd better leave behind some proof."

He plucked a hair from his tail and said, "Change!" The hair turned to a writing brush filled with ink, and Monkey wrote on the pillar,

MONKEY WAS HERE

He returned the hair to his tail, gave another mighty leap, and moments later landed back in the Buddha's palm.

"All right, old monk," said Monkey. "Now keep your part of the bargain and tell the Jade Emperor to clear out."

"You impudent ape!" said the Buddha. "You've been on my palm the whole time!"

"What are you talking about?" said Monkey. "I somersaulted clear to the end of Heaven! If you don't believe me, come see the proof for yourself."

"There's no need to go anywhere," said the Buddha. "Just look down."

Monkey looked down, and there at the base of the Buddha's middle finger were the characters,

MONKEY WAS HERE

"It can't be!" declared Monkey. "It's some kind of trick! I'm going back to look for myself."

But before Monkey could leap again, the Buddha turned his hand over, thrust Monkey out the West Gate of Heaven, and pushed him down to Earth. The hand turned into a five-peaked mountain which pinned Monkey between stone walls. His head and arms were out, but the rest of him was hopelessly trapped.

"You can't do this to me!" cried Monkey. "I'm the Monkey King! I'm an Immortal! I'm the Great Sage Equal to Heaven! Let me out!"

He stopped to consider. Then he added, "Please?"

Epilogue:
To Stone Returned

High above in Heaven, outside the Cloud Palace of the Golden Doors, the Buddha was receiving profuse thanks and congratulations from the Jade Emperor, the Lady Queen Mother, and Lord Lao Tzu. But at last he said, "I must now return to my disciples in the Western Paradise."

He turned to Kwan Yin, Most Compassionate Bodhisattva and Goddess of Mercy. "Would you care to accompany me?"

As the two flew west on magic clouds, Kwan Yin said gently, "No doubt the rebellious Immortal deserved a strict punishment. But wasn't eternal imprisonment a bit harsh?"

"His punishment is not eternal," replied the Buddha. "You may remember I once told you about this very monkey. He is destined to become an enlightened one, a Buddha."

"And how will that come about?" asked Kwan Yin.

"Five hundred years from now," said the Buddha, "I will need a messenger from the Middle Kingdom to come to the Western Paradise and carry back holy scriptures. It will be your own role to find a man or woman worthy of the task. At that time, too, you will recruit our penitent monkey friend to protect the messenger on the long and perilous journey. By doing so, the monkey will atone for his crimes and earn Enlightenment."

"The compassion of the Buddha is beyond measure," said Kwan Yin.

Buddha and Bodhisattva smiled at one another and touched hands lightly. Far ahead, the Temple of the Thunderclap gleamed in the setting sun.

Author Online!

For special features and more stories,
visit Aaron Shepard at

www.aaronshep.com

About the Story

Monkey is the most popular figure in all Chinese literature, loved for centuries by young people and adults alike. His story is found in a classic sixteenth-century novel, *The Journey to the West* (*Xi You Ji* or *Hsi Yu Chi*), as well as in countless later adaptations, from Chinese opera to comic books.

The novel, written anonymously but often attributed to the humorist Wu Cheng'en, is an epic comic fantasy of 100 chapters. My retelling covers only the first seven chapters, which form a kind of prelude. The bulk of the novel recounts the journey of the Buddhist monk Sanzang to collect sacred scriptures from Buddha in the Western Paradise, aided by Monkey and several other magical creatures.

Monkey's adventures provide a breathtaking, whirlwind tour of Chinese mythology, with its rich amalgam of Buddhist and Taoist elements. Here are notes on some of these.

Jade Emperor, Heaven. Though the Jade Emperor is ruler of Heaven and Earth, he is not so much a supreme God as a supreme administrator. In fact, he is outranked by the three top divine beings of the Chinese pantheon, Buddha, Lao Tzu, and Confucius—who are themselves subject to higher universal forces.

The Chinese Heaven is modeled closely on the government of the Chinese emperors. In other words, it is a bloated bureaucracy, crammed with innumerable officials with pompous titles, with a finger in every possible earthly activity.

Lao Tzu, Immortals, Patriarch Subodhi. Centuries before Taoism was established as an organized religion, it existed as a spiritual discipline similar to the yoga systems of India. (*Tao* is pronounced "DOW," rhyming with "cow.") The followers of this branch of Taoism, represented in the story by the Patriarch Subodhi and his disciples, were ascetics living in mountain hermitages. These ascetics aimed to become "Immortals" by developing conscious spirit bodies that could transcend death. But for most Chinese, this was simplified into the belief that Taoist masters achieved *physical* immortality.

The founder of Taoism is said to be Lao Tzu, who became known as a divine being. He is thought to have lived around the 5th or 6th century B.C., though we cannot be sure he actually lived at all. He is also supposed to have written the *Tao Te Ching ("Book of the Way"),* the primary text of Taoism and the most famous of all Chinese classics.

In Taoist literature, secrets of spiritual discipline were often coded in the metaphorical language of alchemy. Most Chinese, though, took this language literally. And so Lao Tzu and other Taoist figures were thought of as master alchemists, producing "Elixir of Life" and "pills of immortality." Cinnabar, or mercuric sulfide—which I've used for the name of Lao Tzu's palace—was a prime ingredient in such "alchemy."

Buddha, Bodhisattva, Western Paradise. *Buddha,* or *the Buddha,* is the title given to Siddhartha Gautama, founder of Buddhism, now revered as a divine being. He lived in India from around 563 to around 483 B.C.

The title means "Enlightened One" or "Awakened One." As such, it is often applied by Buddhists not only to Siddhartha but to all who attain his state of mind—a state that is said to bring a perception of the true nature of reality and a release from the need for additional lives. *Bodhisattva* is a related title for one who has become enlightened but remains on earth to help others toward that goal.

The Western Paradise is where good Buddhists are taken after death—a congenial place where they can progress more rapidly toward becoming Buddhas themselves. This is the teaching of the "Pure Land" school of Buddhism, which predominates in East Asia. In *The Journey to the West,* the Western Paradise is also the present home of the Buddha and seems to be somewhere in India.

Kwan Yin (or Kuan Yin, or Guan Yin). The Bodhisattva Kwan Yin, commonly called the Goddess of Mercy, is China's favorite divine being—much more widely loved and worshiped than the Buddha, Lao Tzu, Confucius, the Jade Emperor, or any other. Her name means "heeding the cry." She hears and helps all those who cry out to her in need, and also delivers babies to their mothers.

Dragon King of the Eastern Sea. In Chinese mythology, dragons are in most cases benevolent. They live underwater and are found in every good-sized lake and river. They can also fly, as they do while performing their main job, which is to bring rain.

There are four dragon kings, headed by the one in the Eastern Sea. Their magnificent palaces and treasure hordes are legendary.

Yama, Judges of the Dead, Land of Darkness. The Land of Darkness is the Chinese Hell. It is not underground but in a kind of parallel dimension. When people reach their fixed times of death, demon officials arrest their spirits and bring them before Lord Yama, the First Judge of the Dead. If their good deeds balance or outweigh their evil ones, they are sent directly to the Tenth Judge for rebirth. Otherwise, they must first pass before the other judges for punishment of various kinds of wrongdoing.

Especially good spirits might be brought to the Land of Darkness only briefly or not at all. They might be sent to Heaven to receive official posts, or to the Buddhist Western Paradise, or to Mount Kunlun, home of the Taoist Immortals.

Lady Queen Mother. In *The Journey to the West,* the Lady Queen Mother is the wife of the Jade Emperor and lives in Heaven. Elsewhere she is often known as the Queen Mother of the West, ruler of Mount Kunlun, home of the Taoist Immortals. In either case, she tends the orchard where the Immortal Peaches grow.

My retelling simplifies and shortens Monkey's tale but broadly follows the original story line. Here are the translations I consulted:

Monkey, by Wu Ch'êng-ên, translated by Arthur Waley, John Day, New York, 1943; reprinted by Grove, New York, 1958. Abridged.

The Journey to the West, translated and edited by Anthony C. Yu, University of Chicago, Chicago and London, 1977. Four volumes.

Journey to the West, by Wu Cheng'en, translated by W. J. F. Jenner, Foreign Languages Press, Beijing, 1982. Three volumes.

For more about the story, plus other special features, visit my Web site at www.aaronshep.com.

Aaron Shepard

Aaron Shepard is the award-winning author of *King o' the Cats, The Sea King's Daughter, The Legend of Lightning Larry,* and many more picture books from major publishers. His stories also appear often in *Cricket* magazine. Please visit him at www.aaronshcp.com.